Ben M. Baglio

PUPPY PUZZLE

Illustrated by
Paul Howard

Cover illustration by
Chris Chapman

A
LITTLE APPLE
PAPERBACK

SCHOLASTIC INC.
New York Toronto London Auckland Sydney

Special thanks to Helen Magee.
Thanks also to C. J. Hall, B.Vet.Med., M.R.C.V.S., for reviewing
the veterinary material contained in this book.

ISBN 0-590-18740-6

Copyright © 1996 by Ben M. Baglio.
Illustrations copyright © 1996 by Paul Howard.

All rights reserved. Published by Scholastic Inc.,
555 Broadway, New York, NY 10012, by arrangement
with Hodder Children's Books, a division of Hodder Headline.

12 11 10 9 8 7 6 5 4 3 2 1   7 8 9/9 0 1 2/0

Printed in the U.S.A.   40
First Scholastic printing, November 1997

Contents

1

Important News

Mandy Hope raced down the path to Animal Ark, hair flying. Would there be news today? She had been thinking about Molly all through school.

Molly was a black Labrador who was expecting puppies. Mrs. Todd, Mandy's teacher, had smiled when Mandy told her why she was so excited.

"You and your animals, Mandy," she said. "Sometimes I think that's all you think about!"

Mandy grinned. She liked her teacher. Mrs. Todd had a spaniel named Jodie. Mrs. Todd liked animals, too.

Mandy pushed open the front door and raced through the hall to the back of the house, dropping her schoolbag as she ran.

She dashed into Animal Ark. Both of Mandy's parents were vets, and their clinic was attached to the house.

"Hey! What's the hurry?" Jean Knox, the receptionist, called.

"Is there any news?" Mandy said in a rush. "Has Molly had her puppies?"

Jean smiled. "Your mom just came back from Moorcroft," she said. "Why don't you go and ask her all about it?"

Mandy bit her lip. "Is she busy?" she said. "Does she have a patient with her?"

Jean shook her head. "No," she said. "The

clinic is closed for the day. She's just giving the animals their medicine. You go ahead. Maybe she'll let you give her a hand. She's in the unit."

The unit was where animals could stay if they were too sick to go home.

Mandy shook her head. "I'm not allowed to help with the animals yet," she said. "But Dad says I can start helping out when I'm twelve." She sighed. "Twelve! Three whole years to go!"

Jean grinned. "I thought you were all excited about Molly and her puppies," she reminded her.

"I am," said Mandy. She rushed over to the door of the unit and pushed it open. "Hi, Mom," she said.

Dr. Emily Hope was in the middle of examining a tortoise. But the tortoise didn't seem to want to come out of his shell. "Mandy!" she said. "Guess what?"

"Molly's puppies have arrived!" said Mandy.

Dr. Emily laughed. "Five of them," she said. "And all healthy."

Mandy sighed with relief. She knew her mother had been worried about Molly. Mrs. Lawson at Moorcroft Farm bred Labradors and Molly was one of her best moms. But Molly was getting a bit old for motherhood now and Mrs. Lawson had decided that this was going to be her last litter.

"And is Molly okay?" said Mandy.

Dr. Emily nodded. "She's fine," she said. "And very proud. You'd think she'd never had puppies before."

"When can I see them?" Mandy asked.

"Give Molly a few days," said Dr. Emily. "Let her settle in with her puppies. Then I'll take you up to see them."

"Terrific!" Mandy said.

Moorcroft Farm was about two miles outside Welford, the village where Mandy lived. The farm was high up on the Yorkshire moors and Mandy loved going there. Mandy loved going *anywhere* as long as there were animals to visit.

Dr. Emily turned back to the tortoise just as he popped his head out of his shell.

"Toto is looking a lot better," she said. "Did you give Jill that pamphlet on caring for tortoises?"

Mandy nodded. "Jill really liked it," she said. "She promised to learn it by heart."

Jill Redfern was in Mandy's class at school. Toto was her tortoise, and had nearly died because Jill had let him hibernate too long.

Mandy put her finger very gently on Toto's head. "Hello, Toto," she said. "How are you

feeling today? You're going to see Jill later. She's coming to visit you."

"*Who's* coming over?" said a voice from the door.

Mandy turned as her father came into the unit and dumped his bag on the counter. He had dark hair and a beard and the kind of smile that made you want to smile, too.

"Jill Redfern," Mandy said. Then she remembered the really important news. "Oh, Dad," she said, "Molly's had her puppies!"

Dr. Adam Hope looked across at his wife. "Everything okay?" he said.

Dr. Emily nodded. "Perfect," she replied. "One of the puppies is a bit on the small side, though. He'll need a little extra care."

"But he will be all right, won't he?" Mandy asked anxiously.

Dr. Emily gave Toto a pat and put him back in his cage. "Of course he will," she said. "He just needs someone to love him and take care of him. Mrs. Lawson will find him a good owner."

"What about me?" Mandy said hopefully. "*I* could look after him."

Dr. Adam and Dr. Emily looked at each other.

"You know the rules, Mandy," Dr. Adam said.

Mandy sighed. She loved her parents being vets because it meant there were always animals around. But they were so busy with everyone else's pets, they didn't have time for any of their own.

"What's for dinner?" said Dr. Adam, changing the subject. "I'm starving."

Dr. Emily laughed. "You're going to have to take up jogging if you don't watch out," she said.

Dr. Adam's eyes twinkled. "*After* dinner," he said.

Dr. Emily moved toward the door. "Come along, Mandy," she said. "Aren't you hungry?"

"Starving!" said Mandy. "But just let me say good-bye to Toto."

Dr. Emily smiled. "Of course," she said.

Mandy turned to the tortoise.

"I'll miss you when you go home," she said softly to the little animal. "But you're going to be well looked after from now on, Toto."

Dr. Emily stood by the door waiting for her.

"You really do love animals, don't you, Mandy?" she said.

Mandy nodded and smiled up at her mother. "Of course I do," she said. "More than anything. And I want to be just like you and Dad when I grow up. I want to be a vet, too."

Her mom smiled. "Let's wait and see," she said. "It'll be a long time before you're grown up. You might change your mind!"

Mandy didn't say anything. But she knew she wouldn't ever change her mind. There was nothing in the world as important to her as animals.

2

Puppy Wanted

The next day Mandy was so eager to tell every-body about Molly's puppies that she raced across the playground without looking where she was going. As she turned the corner of the school building she banged straight into some-one coming from the opposite direction.

"Ouch!" said Mandy, rubbing her nose.

"Ow!" said a voice and Mandy looked down.

A boy was sitting on the ground, rubbing his head. A pair of glasses hung from one ear.

"Sorry," said Mandy. "I was running too fast."

The boy looked up and put his glasses back on. "So was I," he said. "Is your nose all right?"

Mandy gave it another rub. "I don't think it's broken," she said.

The boy grinned. "You're Mandy Hope, aren't you?" he said. "From Animal Ark."

Mandy looked at him. "I know you," she said. "You've got a cat named Benji." She frowned. "The only thing is I can't remember *your* name."

"James Hunter," said the boy, standing up. "I'm in the class below you — Mrs. Black's class."

Mandy was thinking. "Benji had an eye infection last month, didn't he?" she said.

James nodded. "Your dad gave him some drops and he's fine now."

Mandy smiled. "I'm glad," she said.

James had his glasses on properly now. If he was in the class below her, he must be about eight years old. He had brown hair that flopped over his eyes and his glasses were already beginning to slide down his nose. He pushed them back up again.

"So why were you in such a rush?" asked Mandy.

James shook his hair out of his eyes. "I was in a hurry to get to the bulletin board," he said. "I have something to put up."

"What?" asked Mandy.

"An ad," James said.

The news bulletin board was terrific. It was a big pin board on the wall of the main school hall, but you could put all sorts of messages on it. So, if you wanted to sell your bike, or if you'd gotten an award, you could let everybody know.

The main hall was going to have some building work done to it this year. Mandy hoped they wouldn't lose the bulletin board. It was a

12

great way of finding out what was going on in Welford.

"That's where *I* was going," said Mandy. "I have some news as well."

Just then the bell rang and Mandy and James looked at each other.

"Come on," said Mandy. "We'll just have time to put up our ads if we hurry!"

They raced around to the front door of the school and into the main hall. As usual there was a crowd around the bulletin board. Mandy and James had to squeeze past several people to get near it.

"Come on, Mandy," Jill said as she hurried past. "You'll be late."

"This will only take a second," Mandy said.

Jill looked back over her shoulder. "How was Toto this morning?" she asked.

"Mom says you can take him home tomorrow," Mandy said. "She was really impressed when I told her how much you knew about tortoises."

Jill yelled "Yippee!" and raced off down the corridor.

Mandy grinned. Jill must have done an awful lot of work. When she came around to Animal Ark last night, Jill knew everything perfectly. Mandy thought she must be able to recite that tortoise information pamphlet in her sleep now.

Mandy unzipped her schoolbag and pulled out the ad she had written. She put it up on the board and stood back, looking at it.

CONGRATULATIONS TO MOLLY,
THE BEST LABRADOR
IN THE WORLD.
FIVE PUPPIES!
ALL DOING WELL.

The bell stopped ringing and James made a face. "I'll get in trouble with Mrs. Black if I'm late again," he said. He pushed a pin into the bulletin board and looked at his ad. "There," he said. "Got to go. Bye, Mandy!"

"Bye!" said Mandy.

Then James was off, racing down the corridor. He looked back. "Nice running into you," he joked.

But Mandy wasn't listening. She was looking at the notice James had put up.

WANTED
PUPPY
GOOD HOME
CONTACT JAMES HUNTER

Mandy stared at the notice for a moment. Then she turned and looked for James. He was already halfway along the corridor, heading for his classroom.

"James!" she called.

He looked around.

"Meet me here at recess," she shouted.

James looked puzzled.

"Why?" he called back.

"I just had the most terrific idea!" said Mandy.

3

The Best of Friends

Mandy could hardly wait for recess. She rushed out into the playground as soon as the bell rang.

"Hi, James!" she yelled as James came across from the other side of the playground.

"Well?" he said, coming over. "What's your wonderful idea? I'm dying to know!"

"It's about your puppy," Mandy said.

James looked puzzled. "I haven't got a puppy," he said. "That was what my ad was about. I *want* a puppy. Mom and Dad have promised to buy me one. But I don't have one yet."

"I know," said Mandy. "But you didn't see the notice *I* put up, did you?"

James shook his head. "No — what was it about?" he said.

"You know Mrs. Lawson at Moorcroft Farm?" Mandy asked.

James thought for a moment. "Oh, yes," he said. "She breeds dogs, doesn't she?"

Mandy nodded. "She breeds Labradors. And Molly, one of her Labradors, has just had a litter of puppies."

She looked at James, her eyes sparkling. "Mrs. Lawson will be looking for good homes for them. How would you like an adorable Labrador puppy, James?"

James looked at her for a moment, then he grinned. "I'd love one," he said. "A Labrador!

Do you think she would really let me have one?"

Mandy smiled. "I'm sure she would," she said. "I'm going up to Moorcroft with Mom to see the puppies soon. Why don't you come along and have a look at them?"

James's eyes lit up. "Could I?" he said.

Mandy nodded. "You could see if you like any of them," she said.

"And you could help me choose," James said. "You know so much about animals, Mandy."

Mandy shook her head. "Not *that* much," she said. "But I'm learning. I've got all sorts of books about animals. And I'd love to help you choose a puppy."

"Maybe I could borrow a book about Labradors," James said shyly.

Mandy smiled. "Of course you can," she said. "Come over to Animal Ark after school and I'll lend you one."

By the time the bell rang for the end of recess, Mandy and James had made a plan.

"Mom!" Mandy called, rushing into Animal Ark after school.

"In here," her mother called back.

Mandy dumped her schoolbag and raced into the kitchen. She loved the kitchen at Animal Ark. It had oak beams and bright red curtains on the windows. And there was a huge pine table in the middle of the room. Dr. Emily was sitting at it with Mandy's grandmother.

"Oh, hi, Grandma," Mandy said, her eyes

lighting up. She looked at the plate of cookies on the table. "Did you make those?"

Grandma's eyes twinkled. "I certainly did," she said. "They're newly baked this afternoon. Come and have one."

"Not before you've washed your hands," said Dr. Emily.

Mandy went to the sink. "Oh, Mom, you'll never guess," she said. "James Hunter's parents want to buy him a puppy and I told him about Molly. Can he come with us to see the puppies and choose one? I said he could and he's coming in a little while to see what you think. *And* I've promised to lend him a book on Labradors. Don't you think it would be *wonderful* if he took one? Then we'd have one of Molly's puppies living right here in our town!"

"Heavens!" said Grandma. "You're like a runaway train."

Dr. Emily laughed. "Have a glass of milk, Mandy," she said. "And why don't you try all that again? What's this about James Hunter and a puppy?"

Mandy sat down at the table and poured herself some milk from the big blue and white striped pitcher. Grandma put a plate with some cookies on it in front of her.

"Now," said Grandma, "why don't you start at the beginning?"

Mandy took a deep breath and went through the story again.

"I think that's a great idea," Dr. Emily said when she had finished. "Tell James he's welcome to come to Moorcroft with us."

The doorbell rang and Mandy jumped up. "I will," she said. "That must be him now. He only stopped home to tell his mom he was coming here."

Grandma and Dr. Emily looked at each other. "Just as well I made a double batch of cookies then, isn't it?" Grandma said as Mandy ran to let James in.

James came into the kitchen, looking earnestly at Dr. Emily.

"Mandy has told us all about your getting a puppy, James," Dr. Emily said. "Now, sit down and have some cookies and a glass of milk and tell me when you'd like to go to Moorcroft."

"Oh, as soon as possible!" James said eagerly. He sat down beside Mandy at the table.

Grandma laughed. "Just like Mandy," she said. "Always in a hurry."

James flushed. "Oh, sorry," he said. "I mean, whenever you think."

Dr. Emily looked at him. "But the sooner the better?" she said gently.

James smiled up at her. "Oh, yes," he said. "You don't know how much I want a puppy of my own. My parents want one, too. The sooner the better!"

Grandma looked at Mandy and James sitting side by side at the table. "Something tells me you two are going to become the best of friends," she said.

"We already are," Mandy said. "James loves animals. So of *course* we're the best of friends!"

4

A Puppy for James

At the school assembly the next day Mandy sat down next to Sarah Drummond. Sarah was in her class. James was sitting behind them. He leaned over and spoke to Mandy.

"I've been reading that book you gave me," he said. "It's going to be great having a puppy!

I think Labradors are the smartest dogs in the world."

"Are you getting a puppy?" said Sarah. "So am I."

Mandy turned to her. "I didn't know you liked dogs," she said.

Sarah put her nose in the air. "This isn't just *any* puppy," she said. "It's a pedigree."

Mandy bit her lip. "*All* puppies are special," she said. "It doesn't matter whether they're crossbreeds or pedigrees. They're all animals."

"Shh!" said James. "Listen!"

Mandy looked up. Mrs. Garvie, the principal, was standing on the platform at the front of the hall.

"Before you go to class," she said, "I have an announcement to make. We've decided that the last day of the semester will be Pet Day."

There was a murmur of voices as the students turned to one another excitedly.

Mrs. Garvie held up her hand for silence. "All of you will be able to bring your pets to school on that day." She smiled. "Just as long as we don't have any *dangerous* animals."

"Like tigers," said Peter Foster from the row in front of Mandy.

"No tigers, please, Peter. Timmy will be enough of a handful!" Mrs. Garvie said and everybody laughed.

Peter turned bright red.

Timmy was Peter's cairn terrier, and he was the naughtiest dog in town.

"Oh, excellent!" said James. "I'll be able to bring my new puppy."

Sarah looked at him. "And I'll be able to bring *mine*," she said. "I bet mine will be nicer than yours." She looked at Mandy. "Do *you* have a pet?"

Mandy suddenly felt sad. "No," she said. "I don't have a pet of my own."

Sarah looked surprised. "Really," she said. "Imagine living at Animal Ark and not having a pet! I feel sorry for you."

Mandy bit her lip. Sarah didn't *sound* sorry

for her. But Mandy didn't say anything to Sarah.

Mrs. Garvie warned the children to keep out of the way of the builders who were coming to work on the auditorium. Then she announced the end of the assembly. Everyone got up to go.

"Sarah doesn't really feel sorry for me," Mandy said to James as they filed out of the room.

James looked at Mandy. "Don't be upset about Sarah," he said. "She didn't mean it."

Mandy tried to smile, but she still felt sad. "Sometimes I wish I had a pet of my own," she said.

James smiled. "You've got a whole ark full of pets!" he said. "Maybe your mom and dad would let you bring one of *them*?"

Mandy shook her head. "Oh, no," she said, "they wouldn't let me do that. All the animals at Animal Ark are patients."

"Oh," said James.

Mandy smiled. "But *you'll* have a pet to

bring," she said. "You'll have your very own puppy by the end of the semester!"

"It's not far now," said Dr. Emily as the car swung around a bend on the road to Moorcroft Farm.

James was trying to look relaxed, but Mandy could see that he was really excited and nervous.

Dr. Emily looked round. "I hope Benji won't be jealous when you bring a puppy home," she said.

James looked worried. "Do you think he will be?" he asked.

Dr. Emily shrugged. "Maybe you should keep him away from the puppy for a little while," she said. "Benji's bound to be protective of his own territory. After all, he's been the only pet in your house for a long time now. But they'll soon get used to each other."

"I hope so," said James. "I wouldn't like Benji to feel bad."

"He won't," said Mandy. "Just make sure you don't ignore him when the new puppy arrives."

"You might even have to pay more attention to him than you usually do," said Dr. Emily.

"That's no problem," James said. "I like playing with Benji."

The car turned onto the road that led to Moorcroft.

"Oh, look," said Mandy, pointing to a car parked in the farmyard. "That isn't Mrs. Lawson's car. I wonder whose it is."

"Maybe someone else has come to look at the puppies," Dr. Emily said.

Dr. Emily stopped the car and Mandy and James jumped out.

"Let's go see," said Mandy. She raced across the farmyard toward the house.

"Wait for me!" James called, running after her.

"Mrs. Lawson, we're here!" Mandy shouted, knocking on the back door.

Mrs. Lawson came to meet them. She was a friendly-looking lady with gray hair and an old tweed skirt.

"So I see," she said, smiling. "Come on into

the back kitchen. Molly's there with her puppies. And don't make too much noise. She's already had one visitor today."

Mandy immediately clapped a hand to her mouth. "Sorry," she whispered. "Are the puppies asleep?"

Mrs. Lawson grinned. "They're only a few days old," she said. "Puppies that age are usually asleep — when they aren't eating, that is."

Mandy and James tiptoed after her into the farmhouse's warm kitchen.

"There you are," said Mrs. Lawson.

Mandy and James looked where she was pointing. A big wicker basket was next to the bright red stove and Molly was curled up in it. As she lifted her head toward them Mandy got her first glimpse of the puppies, snuggled up close to their mother.

"Oh, look, James!" she said, walking softly across the floor toward the basket. "Aren't they wonderful?"

James came and stood beside her, looking down at the puppies. Five tiny balls of black fur were curled up against their mother. One of them yawned and Mandy could see his little pink tongue. But he kept his eyes closed tightly.

"Their eyes won't open for another week yet," said Mrs. Lawson.

"Oh, look," said Mandy. "Look at that tiny one, the one that just yawned. Isn't he sweet!"

Mrs. Lawson came to stand beside her. "I was worried about him at first," she said. "But he's a strong little fellow. He's going to be all right."

"Is that the one Mom was talking about?" said Mandy. "The smallest one of the litter?"

Mrs. Lawson nodded. "He might be little but he's a real character," she said. "He's got a really friendly nature."

"Are we allowed to touch the puppies?" James asked.

Mrs. Lawson smiled. "Of course," she said.

James bent down and gazed at the smallest puppy. He stretched out a finger and touched the puppy very gently. The little animal gave a tiny squeak.

"Did you hear that?" said James. "He said hello."

Mrs. Lawson laughed. "He certainly did, James."

James turned with a giant grin on his face to Mandy. "I know which one I want," he said.

"Just as long as it's not the one I want!" said a voice from the door.

Mandy and James turned around. Sarah Drummond was standing there.

"My mom wants to have a word with you, Mrs. Lawson," she said.

Mrs. Lawson nodded and walked toward the door.

"Are you adopting one of Molly's puppies, too?" Mandy asked Sarah.

Sarah nodded. "I'm getting the biggest one," she said. "He's beautiful."

James smiled. "That's okay then," he said. "The one I want is the smallest of them all."

Mrs. Lawson looked back at him from the doorway. "Are you sure?" she said. "He'll be a little more work than a big one. You'll need to feed him more often, for starters."

"How often?" asked Mandy.

"Five times a day to begin with," said Mrs. Lawson. "Puppies need lots of milk and high protein food to help them grow."

James looked worried. "How will I know what kind of food to give him?" he said.

"I'll give you a diet sheet," said Mrs. Lawson. "Puppies aren't so very different from human babies. They need just as much care and attention. You start them off on milk and then go on to a little cereal. And after that you can introduce some fish and meat scraps. But they *are* a lot of work. Are you sure you can handle it?"

James pushed his glasses up his nose and nodded. "I'm sure," he said. "And this is the puppy I want. I couldn't have any other. He's perfect."

"And I'll help James look after him," said Mandy.

Mrs. Lawson smiled. "Well, good for you, James," she said. "I think you've made a very good choice there." And she went out of the room.

Sarah looked down into the basket. "*That* little thing!" she said. "Wait until Pet Day. I bet my puppy is twice as big as yours by then!"

Mandy turned to her and smiled. "They'll both be adorable," she said.

But Sarah shook her head. "Mine will be much nicer," she said. "And *you* won't even have a pet to bring to Pet Day."

Mandy's face fell and James stepped forward. "Oh, yes she will," he said.

Sarah and Mandy looked at him in surprise.

"You know I won't," Mandy said.

"What pet?" said Sarah.

James looked down at the puppy he had chosen.

"My puppy," he said. "Mandy is going to help me look after him. We'll share him. We'll both bring him to Pet Day."

Sarah looked annoyed, but Mandy smiled and gave James a grateful look.

"Oh, James," she said. "Are you sure? Can I really share the puppy with you?"

"Of course you can," James said. "How am I going to learn to look after him without your help?"

Mandy looked down at Molly. "There, Molly," she said. "I'm going to be looking after one of your puppies. Isn't that great?"

"Sharing a pet!" said Sarah. "Who ever heard of that?" And she stomped out the door.

5

A New Home

Mrs. Lawson would not let the puppies leave their mother until they were six weeks old. But she told Mandy and James they could come and see their puppy as often as they liked. Mr. Hunter took Mandy and James to see him every week.

The puppy opened his eyes when he was ten

days old and by the end of the second week he was beginning to cut his first teeth. James could hardly wait to get him home.

"I know what I'm going to call him," he said at the end of their second visit.

"What?" said Mandy.

"Blackie," James said.

Mandy looked down at the little black bundle of fur.

"That's perfect, James," she said.

Mr. Hunter smiled. "That's a good name," he said. "You'll need to get him used to it as soon as possible."

"That's true," Mrs. Lawson said. "It's never too early to get a puppy used to his name. Try it out on him now, James."

James bent down and tickled his puppy under the chin. The little dog yawned and looked up at him sleepily.

"Hello, Blackie," James said. "How do you like your name?"

Blackie yawned again and snuggled closer to his mother. His eyes closed.

"He went back to sleep again!" said Mandy.

"Maybe you should call him Sleepy," Mr. Hunter joked.

James shook his head. "I've made up my mind," he said. "He's Blackie!"

When it was time for Blackie to leave his mother, Dr. Adam took Mandy and James to get him. Dr. Adam was going to check on all the puppies before they went off to their new owners.

Mrs. Lawson had put the puppies in a playpen. They rolled around, chasing one another and having pretend fights. Dr. Adam looked at the little animals tumbling around.

"Which one is yours, James?" he said.

James pointed Blackie out and Dr. Adam watched the puppy for a moment.

"He looks like a good one," he said. "Look how he's playing with the others. He's got plenty of confidence, but he isn't aggressive. He's a fine, lively puppy."

"Have you got owners for all of them, Mrs. Lawson?" Mandy said.

Mrs. Lawson nodded. "All the ones I'm selling," she said. "I had no trouble finding good homes for them. Let me get yours for you, James."

She bent down to pick up a puppy.

"Not that one, Mrs. Lawson," Mandy called out. "That isn't James's."

James came to look. "No," he said. "There's mine. The little one."

"My, my," Mrs. Lawson said. "You're right of course. This one is Sarah's. How silly of me."

She picked up James's puppy and looked at him. "These two are very alike," she said.

"James's puppy really has grown a lot," said Mandy.

"But he's still a *little* smaller," said James.

"I would know your puppy anywhere, James," Mandy said. "Blackie's got such a nice look in his eyes. He's so friendly."

Mrs. Lawson laughed. "You're very obser-

41

vant, Mandy," she said. "I'm glad I didn't get these two mixed up!"

James held out his arms and Mrs. Lawson gave him the puppy. The little animal squeaked and looked up at his new owner. His tiny pink tongue came out and he licked James's hand.

James looked at Mandy. "I can't believe it," he said. "My very own puppy!"

Mandy put out a hand and stroked the puppy's soft coat.

"He's beautiful," she said softly. "The nicest of the litter!"

Dr. Adam looked at Blackie. "You know, I think you're right, Mandy," he said. "Look how easily he lets James handle him. And see the way he's looking back at James. That's the mark of a confident animal."

James cradled Blackie in the crook of his arm. "He's so good-natured," he said.

Dr. Adam nodded. "Turn him on his back, James," he said. "Let's see how he reacts."

James turned Blackie over. The puppy

squirmed a little and then lay contentedly in James's arms.

"There, you see," said Dr. Adam. "That's what you're looking for in a puppy. A bit of a struggle and then he settles down quickly. I'd say you've got a fine puppy there, James."

"Of course he has," Mandy said. "All Molly's puppies are wonderful, aren't they, girl?" She turned to look down at Molly.

The Labrador looked up at her with sad eyes.

"Oh, Molly," Mandy said. "You're going to miss your puppies, aren't you?"

Mrs. Lawson gave Molly a pat. "I'm keeping one of the puppies to breed from," she said. "So Molly won't lose all of her family."

Mandy smiled. It was good to think of Molly still having one of her puppies to look after.

Mr. and Mrs. Hunter were waiting eagerly for them to arrive home with the puppy.

"I've got his bed all ready," said Mrs. Hunter. "Bring him straight into the kitchen."

Mandy followed James and Blackie into the

kitchen. There were newspapers spread out over the kitchen floor.

"Just in case of accidents," Mrs. Hunter said.

Dr. Adam nodded. "Very wise," he said. "You can't always get a puppy of that age outside in time!"

Mandy looked at the dog basket in the corner of the room. There was a cardboard box inside it.

"What's that for?" she said.

"The dog basket is too big for him at the moment," Mr. Hunter said. "But if we put him in a box inside the basket, then he'll get used to it."

"That's a good idea," said Mandy.

"And I put an old blanket in the bottom of the box," said James. "So Blackie will be really cozy."

"If he misses his mother, you could put a hot-water bottle in beside him," said Dr. Adam. "But make sure it has a cover on it."

James nodded. "I'll do that," he said. "I'm sure Blackie will miss Molly."

Blackie looked up at him and gave a soft little growl.

"Did you hear that?" said James. "I think he knows his name already."

"Maybe he's hungry," said Mandy. "Mrs. Lawson said we should give him something to eat when we get him home."

Dr. Adam looked at his watch. "I must get back to the clinic," he said. "Give him something to eat now, James. Some warm milk with cereal and grated vegetables should do. And don't forget to take him outside immediately afterwards. House-training can't begin too soon!"

"Can Mandy stay for dinner?" James asked.

Dr. Adam and the Hunters looked at one another.

"I don't think I could drag her away if I wanted to!" said Dr. Adam, laughing.

Mrs. Hunter looked at Mandy. She and James were already gathering things together for Blackie's feed.

"Something tells me you aren't going to see too much of Mandy for a while," she said to Dr. Adam.

6

An Escape

Mandy went to James's house every day after school. They had tried the hot-water bottle trick and Blackie was settling in well. In fact he was getting very adventurous, starting to explore his new home. Benji the cat was also interested in Blackie. But poor little Blackie was terrified of him. Not that Benji would hurt Blackie. He only wanted to play.

By the time Blackie was ten weeks old there were fewer puddles on the kitchen floor for Mandy and James to mop up and the puppy was eating some solid food. House-training was pretty important so Mandy and James made a big effort.

"We have to find a way of telling him to go outside," said James. "We should use the same words each time so that he'll know what to do."

"And we need to make sure we always take him to the same place in the garden," said Mandy.

"That's okay," James said. "Dad has fenced off a corner especially for him, so as long as we take him out straight after meals there shouldn't be any accidents. But we have to clean up after him."

"Of course we will," said Mandy. "It would be good to get him trained before we start taking him out for walks."

They would be allowed to take him out in three or four weeks — once his shots were completed. But for now, they had to keep him in the garden or carry him if they wanted to take him out of the house.

On Friday evening, Mandy knocked on the Hunters' door as usual.

"James is in the kitchen," Mrs. Hunter said to Mandy.

Mandy made her way to the kitchen and pushed open the door.

"Hi, Mandy!" James said, then looked behind her. "Shut the door," he said. "Quick!"

Mandy turned to close the door, but she was too slow. Benji shot through her legs into the kitchen.

"Oh, no!" she said, making a dive for Benji. "Sorry, James. I forgot."

James darted toward the dog basket, but he was too late. A bundle of black fur scrambled out of the cardboard box and over the side of the basket, skidding across the kitchen floor.

Benji made a dash for the puppy, but the little animal scampered out of the kitchen and down the hall.

"Oh, no!" said James. "Where has he *gone*?"

Mandy groaned. "I left the door open. I'm sorry!"

James made a dive for Benji and gathered him up in his arms. "It's okay," he said. He looked down at Benji. "We know you wouldn't hurt the puppy," he said. "But you do frighten him."

Mandy took Benji into the living room and explained to Mrs. Hunter what had happened.

"Don't you worry, Mandy," Mrs. Hunter

said. "I'll keep Benji here. You two search for Blackie."

Mandy found James in the hall.

"I think he's in there," said James pointing to the closet under the stairs. The door was slightly open.

"If your hall closet is anything like ours, it'll take ages to find him," said Mandy. "But nothing could be as bad as ours."

James pulled open the door. The closet was filled with golf clubs and tennis rackets, umbrellas and boxes, and all *sorts* of things.

"I take that back," said Mandy. "It's even *worse* than ours!"

"Mom is always saying we need to clear it out," James said.

"Oh, well, let's take a look with the light on," said Mandy.

James shook his head. "There isn't a light," he said. "Dad is always meaning to put one in."

Mandy peered into the deep recesses of the closet. "How are we going to find a black puppy in a pitch-black closet?" she said.

James pushed his glasses up on to his nose. "We'll just have to move all this stuff until we find him," he said.

"Or lure him out," said Mandy. "I'll go and get him something to eat."

"Good idea," said James, lifting a golf bag out of the closet. "Here, Blackie!" he called hopefully.

By the time Mandy got back with a bowl of milk James had dragged a pile of stuff out of the closet. But there was still no sign of the puppy.

Mandy put the bowl down on the floor. Then she and James crouched down and waited. There was a scuffling noise at the back of the cupboard, then the scratching of tiny nails. Very slowly a small black head peered out from behind a cardboard box.

Mandy held her breath. She didn't want to scare Blackie. The puppy sniffed gently at the side of the cardboard box, then crept around it, sniffing as he caught the scent of milk. Slowly, his eyes flicking from the milk to Mandy and

James, he crept closer until he was beside the bowl.

Mandy and James stayed perfectly still until Blackie put his head down and began to lap. James let him polish off all the milk before he scooped him up into his arms and cuddled him.

"Bad Blackie!" he said.

Mandy grinned. "At least he got an extra snack," she said. "If that happens very often, he'll soon put on weight."

James looked at the puppy proudly. "He *is* getting bigger, isn't he?" he said. "Soon he'll be as big as Sarah's puppy."

"Licorice," said Mandy.

"Is that what she named him?" James asked. "Of course, he's as black as Blackie."

Mandy gave Blackie a pat. "I wonder if he gets into as much mischief as Blackie does," she said. Then she laughed. "He was completely invisible in that dark closet. You certainly picked the right name for him, James."

James tickled the puppy under the chin. "Oh, Blackie," he said. "What *will* you do next?"

7

"Sit!"

Mandy looked up from the book she was reading. It was called *You and Your Dog*.

She looked across the Hunters' kitchen table at James. James also had his nose buried deep in a book. Blackie was curled up fast asleep in his basket.

"You know, James," she said, "it's time to

start thinking about Blackie's obedience train-ing. After all, he's twelve weeks old now."

James looked up from his book. "I know," he said. "But how can we train him with Benji around? Blackie still runs away every time he sees Benji."

"We could take him to Animal Ark," Mandy said.

James shook his head. "Blackie hasn't had all his shots yet," he said. "We can't let him come in contact with other animals in case he picks up an infection. There are too many animals coming in and out of the clinic. We need somewhere quiet with no other animals."

"And somewhere that Blackie can't get out of," said Mandy.

"He's good at getting out of places," James said. "He nearly got out of the garden yester-day."

The back door opened and Mrs. Hunter came in just in time to hear James's last words. "I tore a new pair of tights scrabbling in the hedge to catch him," she said.

Blackie stirred and sat up, blinking at the sound of James's mother's voice.

"Now, don't you go getting into any more mischief," Mrs. Hunter scolded him.

The front doorbell rang. Mrs. Hunter put her shopping basket down on the floor and went out to answer the door.

Mandy was still thinking about Blackie's training. "We could take him to Grandma's and Grandpa's," she said. "Grandpa has just put a new fence all around their garden. Even Blackie couldn't get out of it."

James pushed his book aside, looking hopeful. Blackie scrambled out of his basket and scampered across the floor. "That's a great idea," James said. Then he looked at Blackie. "Oh, no!" he said. "Blackie, *no!*"

The little dog was tugging at a paper bag in Mrs. Hunter's shopping basket. The bag burst open and several cream pastries rolled across the floor. Blackie pounced on one of them and began licking up the cream.

The kitchen door opened before Mandy or James could get to Blackie.

"What on earth . . . ?" began Mrs. Hunter, as she came back in. Then she looked at James. "It's about time that puppy started learning how to behave himself!" she said.

James looked at Mandy. "Are you sure your grandma and grandpa would let us train Blackie at their house?"

Mandy smiled. "Of course they would," she said. "They'd love it. Just you wait and see."

"Sit!" James said sternly.

It was Saturday and Mandy and James were in the back garden of Lilac Cottage, Mandy's grandparents' house.

Blackie looked up at James and wagged his tail.

"Maybe if you pushed his bottom down at the same time as you said 'sit'," suggested Mandy.

James looked at her in despair. "I've tried that," he said.

Mandy bit her lip. They'd been trying to train Blackie for two weeks now and were getting nowhere.

The little puppy looked eagerly at them, jumping up and resting his paws against James's jeans. Mandy moved a few yards away and looked at Blackie.

"Stay!" she said in a firm voice.

Blackie immediately ran toward her.

"It's hopeless," said Mandy, laughing. "I don't think we'll ever train him!"

"Licorice always sits when I tell him to," said a voice behind them.

"Sarah!" said Mandy, turning around.

Sarah was standing at the back garden gate with Licorice in her arms.

"Does he really sit when you tell him to?" asked James, coming over. "Let's see. I don't know how you get him to do as he's told."

Sarah drew back, cradling Licorice in her arms. "I can't," she said. "Not here. He's still got one more bunch of shots to take and I'm not allowed to put him down outside until he's had all of them."

Mandy nodded. "Blackie gets his final bunch next week," she said. "We had to carry him all the way here. But he can run around in the garden. It's safe here."

Sarah put her nose in the air. "Run around is right," she said. "Where has he gone?"

Mandy and James looked around.

"Blackie!" James called. "Blackie, where are you?"

"Huh!" said Sarah. "He doesn't even answer to his name. Just you wait and see what

59

Licorice can do at Pet Day." And she walked off down the street.

Mandy and James looked at each other.

"Where is he?" said Mandy.

Grandpa came around the side of the garden shed.

"Oh, Grandpa, have you seen Blackie?" asked Mandy.

"I certainly have. He was in my raspberry bushes," Grandpa said.

Mandy looked up at him. "Oh, no!" she said.

Grandpa's eyes twinkled. "It's all right," he said. "I caught him before he did any harm."

"But where is he now?" said James.

Grandpa rubbed his nose. "Mandy's grandma has him in the house," he said. "She really likes the little one."

Mandy smiled. "I knew it was a good idea to bring him to Lilac Cottage," she said.

"So how is the training going?" Grandpa asked.

Mandy and James looked at one another.

"It isn't very easy," James said.

"Blackie looks at us with those big brown eyes of his," Mandy said.

"And you can't bear to scold him?" Grandpa said.

Mandy nodded. "He's such a sweetie," she said.

Grandpa grunted. "If he gets in among my raspberry bushes again he won't be a sweetie to me," he said.

Mandy bit her lip. She knew Grandpa didn't mean it. He was just as fond of Blackie as Grandma was. But she and James didn't seem to be making much progress with Blackie's training. Maybe they weren't being firm enough with him.

The back door opened and Grandma popped her head out.

"Come and see this," she said. "You won't believe it!"

Mandy and James rushed to the door with Grandpa following. Blackie was sitting in the middle of the kitchen floor.

"What is it?" said James.

Then Mandy realized. Blackie wasn't running around or trying to chew anybody's
shoelaces. He was just sitting there.

"I told him to sit," Grandma said proudly.

"And he did?" said James. "Mrs. Hope,
you're amazing!"

Grandma shook her head and smiled. "It's all
done by kindness," she said.

Mandy looked at Blackie. "Good boy," she
said. "Wait until Sarah sees *this* at Pet Day!"

Blackie gave a short bark and scampered off
out of the back door.

"My raspberry bushes!" Grandpa shouted. The four of them raced after Blackie, until Mandy, flushed bright red, caught him and gathered him up into her arms.

"What that little one needs is a leash and collar!" Grandpa said.

Mandy looked at her grandpa. "But he's so young," she said.

Grandpa was firm. "Fourteen weeks isn't too young for a leash and collar," he said. "You're going to be able to take him out for walks soon. You'll need to have him on a leash then."

"That's right," said James.

"Mrs. McFarlane at the general store had some nice dog collars last week," said Grandma.

Mandy smiled at her. "Then that's where we'll go," she said. "We'll do that this afternoon."

The general store was Mandy's favorite shop in the village. You could get almost anything there — comics and candy, books and puzzles.

The shelves were piled high with all kinds of things.

Mandy pushed open the door and she and James went inside.

"Well," said Mrs. McFarlane. "What can I do for you two?"

Then she saw Blackie in James's arms. "My, my," she said. "What a beautiful puppy!"

James beamed with pride as Mrs. McFarlane came around from behind the counter to admire Blackie.

"We want a leash and collar for him," said Mandy.

Mrs. McFarlane smiled. "And I have just the thing," she said. "I've got a beautiful red leather one that would suit him well. And I can make him a tag with your address and phone number on it, James."

She took a collar and leash down from a hook and handed them to James.

"They're great," Mandy said.

James looked at the collar doubtfully. "It won't hurt him, will it?" he said.

Mrs. McFarlane shook her head. "Not a bit," she replied. "It would hurt him a lot more if he got away from you and ran into the road and got hit by a car."

"That's true," said Mandy.

James made up his mind. "We'll take them," he said.

Mandy helped him fasten the collar around Blackie's neck and clip on the leash.

It wasn't easy. Blackie wiggled and squirmed and scratched at the collar with his paws.

"He doesn't like it," said James.

Mandy looked down at the little puppy. He was looking up at her and his big brown eyes looked sad.

"But he has to wear it," she said.

James looked at his pet. "I suppose so," he said.

Mrs. McFarlane smiled at them. "He'll get used to it soon," she said. "Just make sure you keep it on him when you're walking him. He's far too young to be off the leash yet if he isn't somewhere safe."

Mandy nodded, but James was still looking worried.

"Come on, James," she said. "Let's take him home and try walking him on the leash to see if he gets used to it."

But when they got back to James's house and set Blackie down in the garden, he didn't seem to like the collar at all. He kept scratching and tugging at it until James picked him up and gave him a hug.

"He really does have to get used to it," Mandy said gently. "It will take some time."

James looked at her. She could see he was upset. "Maybe the collar is too tight," he said. "Maybe if I loosened it a little he wouldn't mind so much."

"Maybe," said Mandy. "But don't loosen it so much that he can slip out of it."

James nodded, but he didn't look convinced.

Mandy knew it was very hard to train a puppy. Sometimes it seemed very cruel. But she was sure James would get used to training Blackie — and that Blackie would get used to being trained.

8

Pet Day

It felt like Pet Day would never come. But, at last, the final day of the semester arrived. Mandy and James arranged to meet before school and take Blackie to the big day together.

"Oh, look, there's Jill with Toto," Mandy said as she and James came through the school gates. Jill was carrying her tortoise in a small cardboard box with an airhole cut into it.

Blackie was running around, twisting his leash around James's legs.

"Heel!" said James, pulling on the leash.

Blackie looked up at him and sat down on James's feet.

James sighed. "I don't think we'll ever be able to train him," he said.

Mandy laughed. "Of course we will," she said. "He's only four months old." She looked up. "Here comes Jill!"

Jill waved and rushed over to them. "Look how well Toto looks, Mandy," she said. Then she saw Blackie. "Oh, James, he's gorgeous!"

Blackie stood up and wagged his tail so hard he nearly fell over. James swelled with pride. "I know," he said. "You'd never believe how much he's grown in the last few weeks. He was tiny when I first got him."

"He still isn't as big as Licorice," said a voice behind them. Mandy turned around. Sarah was

standing there with a coal black Labrador puppy in her arms.

"Hello, Licorice," Mandy said, tickling the puppy under the chin.

"Look, Blackie," James said to his puppy. "That's your brother!"

Sarah looked at Blackie. "Your *big* brother," she said.

Mandy looked from Blackie to the puppy in Sarah's arms. "I don't know about that," she said. "They look pretty much the same size to me."

"And they're so alike," said Jill. "Don't get them mixed up. You wouldn't be able to tell them apart!"

"*I* would," said James. "I'd know Blackie anywhere."

"And so would I," said Mandy.

Sarah sniffed. "As if anybody could mistake my perfect little puppy for James's," she said, sweeping past them. "His was the runt of the litter!"

Mandy looked at James's face.

"Don't pay any attention to her," Mandy said.

"She's probably just jealous of Blackie's red collar and leash," said Jill. "Her puppy doesn't have a collar. She'll have to carry him everywhere."

James looked more cheerful. "We've already started to train Blackie," he said.

"Does he know any tricks?" asked Jill.

"Not really," said James. "But he's still very young."

Mandy smiled. That was better. Poor James had looked really upset before. Sarah was the kind of person that was hard to stand up to.

"Come on," Mandy said. "Let's go and see everyone else's pets. I can't wait!"

Mandy looked around the classroom. The walls were covered with posters of animals. There was a big display in the corner with photographs of everyone's pets and a table full of animal books. All around her, people were sitting with their animals in their cages or baskets or boxes.

There was Jill and Toto, of course. Then Peter with Timmy, the terrier. There were several rabbits, two guinea pigs, three hamsters, and a parrot. There was a hedgehog, a gerbil, two cats, four kittens, and a canary. And Gary Roberts was giving a speech about snakes. Mandy was in heaven!

"It'll be your turn soon," she whispered to James.

James turned to her. "*Our* turn, you mean," he said. "I'm not standing up in front of everyone alone. I'd be way too nervous."

Mrs. Todd and Mrs. Black had joined their two classes together. Everyone who brought a pet was giving a little talk about taking care of their animals.

Gary had a snake draped over his arm. He held it up to let the class see the pale yellow stripes on its greenish-black skin.

"What does it eat?" asked Amy Fenton, holding on to the cage with her pet mouse in it.

"Mostly worms and tadpoles," Gary said.

Amy looked suspicious. "Not mice?" she asked.

Gary shook his head. "No," he said. "Garter snakes don't eat mice."

"And you're sure he isn't dangerous?" said Amy.

"No, of course he isn't dangerous," Gary said to Amy. "He's a garter snake, not a python or a cobra."

"Amy is worried about Minnie," whispered Mandy, looking at Amy's mouse.

James smiled. "She should look out for Richard Tanner's cat then," he said.

Mandy looked across the room at Duchess, Richard's enormous Persian cat.

"She really suits her name," Mandy said as Duchess yawned and gazed around the classroom as if she owned it.

"Thank you, Gary," Mrs. Todd said as he went to sit down. "Now, I see we have two little puppies here today." She smiled at James and Sarah. "Who's going to go first?" she asked.

"I will," said Sarah eagerly. "I want to show you what Licorice can do."

Sarah carried Licorice out to the front of the class and put him down on the floor.

"Sit!" she instructed the puppy.

The puppy gave a short bark and wagged his tail. He didn't make the slightest move to sit.

"See," said Mandy. "Blackie isn't the only disobedient one."

"Sit!" Sarah said again to Licorice.

Licorice lay down and rolled over to have his tummy tickled.

"Oh, he's so cute," said Amy Fenton.

Sarah looked around the class. "He *can* do it," she said. "He *can* sit when I tell him. Sit, Licorice!"

Mrs. Todd smiled. "I'm sure he can do it, Sarah," she said. "But he's probably too excited with all the other animals here today."

Sarah looked really upset as she bent to pick Licorice up. Mandy felt sorry for her.

"Blackie is the same way," she said.

"That's right," said James. "He does just as he likes, whatever we say!"

Sarah looked around. "Does he?" she said. "Really?"

"You bet," said James.

"Tell everyone about the pastries," said Mandy.

"Yes, tell us about the pastries, James," said Mrs. Black. "That sounds interesting."

James stood up and told the story about Blackie and the cream pastries. Mandy looked at him, amazed. Usually James was quite shy. But soon he had the whole class laughing. Even Sarah cheered up.

"I thought you were too nervous to talk to the class," Mandy whispered as he sat down.

James blushed. "I *was*," he said. "But I forgot all about that when I started talking about Blackie."

The bell rang for the end of school and everyone groaned.

"My goodness," said Mrs. Todd. "I've never seen you all so disappointed that it was time to go home. *Especially* on the last day of school!"

"Maybe we should do this more often," Mrs. Black suggested.

"Oh, can we? Please!" said Mandy.

Mrs. Todd looked at her. "You would have animals in the classroom every day if you could, Mandy," she said.

Mandy nodded. "That's right!" she said. "This is the best day I've ever had at school!"

James almost had to drag Mandy away.

"Oh, just a moment," she said. "I haven't said hello to Carrie's parrot. He was really sick last year. Just look at him now!"

James shook his head. "Do you know *all* the animals here?" he said.

Mandy turned to him in surprise. "Yes, I suppose I do," she said. She smiled. "You're right, James. I know them all. Each one has been to Animal Ark at one time or another."

James grinned at her. "You've got more animal friends than anybody I know," he said.

Mandy nodded, her eyes shining. "I may not have a pet of my own," she said. "But I've got a whole village full of animal friends."

In a way she was lucky. Her friends might each have a pet, but she had *lots* of animals to care for.

"You know, James," she said, "I don't think I mind not having a pet!"

James laughed as Timmy, Peter's cairn terrier, ran across the playground and jumped up at Mandy's legs.

"Everybody else's pets come to you," he said.

"Oh, Timmy," said Mandy, bending down to pat the little dog.

James clipped on Blackie's leash and adjusted

his collar. Then he pointed a finger at the little puppy.

"Heel!" he said.

Blackie put his head on one side and looked at James curiously.

Mandy giggled. "Isn't he adorable?" she said.

James grinned. "Yes, he is," he said. "But he isn't very obedient."

Timmy walked over to Blackie and gave a sharp little bark. Blackie backed away. James held onto his leash.

"Timmy is only trying to make friends, Blackie," James said to his puppy.

Blackie looked at the other dog. Then he took a step forward and nudged the terrier with his nose. Timmy snuffled gently and laid a paw on Blackie's back. Blackie growled softly and butted Timmy playfully.

"There," said Mandy. "They're playing!"

There was a shout from the other side of the playground and Mandy turned to look.

"My rabbit! Catch him, quickly," a small girl shouted.

"Oh, no!" said James. "Laura Baker's rabbit has run away!"

Timmy the terrier gave a short sharp bark and shot out of Mandy's reach. He raced across the playground, heading straight for the rabbit.

"Oh, no," said James. He cupped both hands around his mouth. "Timmy!" he called.

"James!" said Mandy. "Watch out!"

But it was too late. James had let go of Blackie's leash and the little puppy was off across the playground before Mandy or James could catch him. The leash trailed behind him as he ran after his new friend. Blackie thought it was a game.

"Oh, no," said James. "Quick! After him, Mandy!"

9

Catch That Rabbit!

Mandy and James raced across the playground. Blackie was far away by now. Mandy lost sight of him as the other children began to chase after Laura's rabbit. The playground was in an uproar.

"Timmy! Come back!" yelled Peter, running across the playground.

He was in such a rush, he didn't see Sarah hurrying toward the school gates with Licorice in her arms.

"Watch out!" Mandy yelled.

But it was too late. Peter and Sarah collided and Licorice jumped out of Sarah's arms. The little puppy stood for a moment, then ran off across the playground and disappeared in the crowd.

Peter barely noticed. He kept running, trying to catch up with Timmy.

"Oh, catch him, catch Licorice!" Sarah shouted as Mandy came up to her. She turned to Mandy. "What if Licorice gets lost or someone steps on him?"

"Don't worry. We'll get him," said Mandy. "Blackie has run away, too."

Sarah looked really angry. "I don't care about Blackie!" she said. "It's Licorice I'm worried about." She looked at her watch. "Mom will be here in a minute to get me. She'll be furious. She hates it if I keep her waiting."

Mandy looked at Sarah's angry expression.

She was only concerned about her own pet and being late for her mom. She didn't care about anyone else.

"Come on!" James shouted as he caught up with Mandy. "I think I saw Blackie heading for the garbage cans."

"It was probably Licorice," said Sarah. "Let me see." And she dashed off.

By this time the playground was full of people running back and forth, trying to catch the loose pets.

Mandy and James ran around the school and into the yard on the other side where the garbage cans were.

"There's Timmy!" Peter cried and ran after the terrier. "Catch him," he yelled to a group of children. They fanned out, forming a half circle. Peter dove for Timmy and caught him.

"Got you!" he said.

"There's the rabbit," said James, darting behind a garbage can.

"Careful, James," Mandy shouted. "Don't scare him or he'll panic."

But James was hot on the trail of Laura's rabbit. He cornered it in the bricked-off area that housed the garbage cans.

"Don't scare him," Mandy said.

James looked at her.

"Maybe you'd better do this," he said.

Mandy knelt down very quietly and held her hand out to the terrified rabbit. The little animal looked at her, its eyes huge with fear.

"There now, Nibbles," Mandy said softly. "There's nothing to be afraid of."

The rabbit wiggled his nose, sniffing the air, then he took a tiny step toward her. Just at that moment a small black puppy ran into view.

"Blackie!" yelled James and the rabbit's ears pricked up.

Mandy moved fast, gathering the rabbit into her arms before it could make another dash away. James tried to catch the puppy. But Sarah was there before him.

"That isn't Blackie," she said, scooping the puppy into her arms. "It's Licorice. Anyone can see *that*!"

Mandy was busy soothing the frightened rabbit.

Laura came up to her, tears running down her face.

"Oh, Nibbles is all right, isn't he?" she said. "He isn't hurt?"

Mandy smiled at her. "He's just a bit frightened," she said. "He'll be fine once you get him home."

Laura took the rabbit carefully from her and headed for the school gates.

Mandy turned to James. "Poor Nibbles," she said. "He got the scare of his life."

But James wasn't listening. He was staring at Sarah.

"How can you be so sure that's Licorice?" he said.

Sarah looked at him scornfully. "Because Blackie had a collar on," she said. "And this puppy doesn't."

Mandy looked at the puppy in Sarah's arms. It certainly looked like Blackie.

"Blackie?" she said.

The little puppy gave a short bark and scrabbled his paws against Sarah's sleeve.

Sarah turned and began to walk away. "I tell you this is Licorice," she said.

Mandy frowned. The puppy did look like Blackie. But maybe Sarah was right. After all, she should know her own puppy! Besides, Blackie had a collar and Licorice didn't.

"Sorry!" she called after Sarah. "It's just that they're so alike."

Sarah sniffed. "I thought you said you would be able to tell the difference," she called back. "You're supposed to know so much about animals."

Mandy blushed. "I've never said that," she said quietly.

There was the sound of a car horn tooting and Sarah ran off toward the school gates and her mother's car.

Mandy looked around. The playground had emptied out. Everyone had found their pets now. Only Mandy and James were left.

Mandy turned to James. He was biting his lip.

"I'm *sure* that was Blackie," he said.

"But Blackie had a collar on," said Mandy.

James looked at her. "I loosened his collar earlier on," he said. "I thought it was too tight."

"So he could have slipped out of it?" said Mandy. "Oh, James, why didn't you say so?"

James looked really worried. "Sarah seemed so sure of herself," he said. "I don't *know* if I'm right. I just *think* I am. She rushed off so fast I didn't really get a chance to get a good look at the puppy."

Mandy felt sorry for him. Sarah always thought she knew best. She was always so sure she was right that she made you believe her.

Mandy looked around. "So where's Licorice?" she said. "If that really *was* Blackie then Licorice must be around here somewhere. All we have to do to solve the puzzle is to find the other puppy. Once we have both, we'll be able to tell the difference."

James saw something lying in the corner of the playground.

"Look," he said, going over and picking it up.

"Blackie's collar and leash!" said Mandy.

"It looks as if I might be right," said James. "Sarah must have taken the wrong puppy home with her."

"That isn't so important at the moment," said Mandy. "At least we know that *one* puppy is safe."

"What do you mean?" said James.

Mandy turned to him, her eyes worried. "James, it doesn't matter which one it is. There's a puppy missing and we have to find him!"

10

A Frightened Puppy

"Where should we start looking?" James said.

Mandy bit her lip.

"I don't know," she said. "I only hope he hasn't managed to get out of the playground."

James looked worried. "Maybe he's hiding somewhere."

Mandy nodded. "If he's scared, that's probably what he'd do," she said.

"Well, he isn't behind the garbage cans," James said.

Mandy's eyes went to the corner of the yard. There was a heap of old floorboards and shelves piled up against the side of the bicycle shed. The workmen had put them there when they were working on the school.

"Look at all that stuff the workmen are throwing out," she said. "You don't think he could have crawled in there?"

"We could check," said James.

Mandy and James ran over to the pile of wooden planks. "Oh, I do hope he isn't in there," Mandy said. "It doesn't look at all safe."

"Listen," said James. "Do you hear something?"

Mandy shook her head.

"I'm sure I heard a sound," said James.

Then Mandy heard it too — a tiny squeak. But it wasn't coming from inside the pile of wood.

She frowned. "It sounds like it's coming from up there." She pointed to the top of the pile.

James looked up, just as a small black face appeared over the edge.

"There he is!" said Mandy.

James swallowed. "But how on earth did he get all the way up there?" he said.

"Frightened animals do the strangest things," Mandy said.

The puppy looked down at them. He put out a paw. The board he was standing on tipped forward slightly.

"Oh, no!" said Mandy, her breath catching in her throat.

"Go back!" James called to the puppy, gesturing with his hands.

The puppy backed off a little but soon stepped forward again, scrabbling at the edge of the board. He barked down at them.

"He's frightened," said Mandy. "He wants to come down."

"But that plank doesn't look too steady," said

James. "If it tips over, he'll fall right into the middle of the pile. He'll get hurt."

Mandy frowned. She looked at the pile of wood. It was built up against the corner of the bike shed where it met the wall that ran around the school yard. The puppy had backed away to the far side of the pile — almost against the wall.

"What are you thinking?" asked James.

Mandy looked at the sloping roof of the shed. "If I could get onto that roof I could walk along the wall and try to reach him," she said.

James looked at the wall that ran along behind the shed. "But it's too narrow," he said. "You'd fall. We'd better try and get help."

Just then the puppy put out a paw and the plank he was on rocked dangerously.

"There isn't time," Mandy said. "You've got to help me, James. I can't get up on the roof on my own."

James looked doubtful.

"Don't worry," said Mandy. "I'll be really careful."

"All right," James said.

Mandy walked toward the shed and James came after her.

"Cup your hands," said Mandy. "Then I can stand on them and climb up onto the roof."

Mandy put her foot into James's cupped hands. "Now lift," she said as she pushed herself up.

James pushed and Mandy grabbed the edge of the shed roof. For a moment she thought she was going to fall, then she got a grip on it and heaved herself up.

"So far so good," she said as she wriggled her way onto the roof. She looked down at James.

"Be careful," he pleaded.

Mandy smiled. "Oh, I will be," she said. "If I'm not careful, I won't be able to rescue the puppy."

Then she walked across the roof and onto the wall. Slowly, carefully, she balanced her way along the wall until she was just opposite the puppy. He turned his big brown eyes toward her.

"It's all right," she said to the puppy. "Nobody is going to hurt you. Come, come to Mandy."

The puppy looked at her. He was quivering with fright. Mandy held her hand out to him, speaking softly but firmly. The little dog began to edge toward her along the plank — away from the dangerous end of it.

"That's right," said Mandy. "Just a few steps more. Come on."

The puppy took another step. He was almost

within reach. Mandy wanted to stretch out and grab him, but she knew that would be the wrong thing to do. If she missed, the puppy would panic and lose his balance. Mandy looked down at the heap of jagged floorboards and shelves and old cupboard doors. She shook her head. She wasn't going to risk it.

The little animal took another step nearer. Mandy held her hand steady. She talked to him all the time in a soothing voice, encouraging him.

"Not far now," she said.

He was almost at her hand. He pressed his wet nose into her palm and sniffed. He gave her hand a little lick.

"Good boy," said Mandy. "Come on, you can do it."

At last, after a long pause, the puppy stepped forward and nuzzled Mandy's sleeve.

Mandy put out both hands and clasped him firmly to her.

"There," she said, gathering him up. "Now you're safe!"

The puppy looked up into her eyes and Mandy frowned. This *had* to be Licorice. He just didn't feel like Blackie.

"Licorice?" she said.

The puppy gave a soft bark as if he recognized his name. But he still seemed a little frightened of Mandy.

Mandy walked very carefully back along the wall and handed the puppy down to James. The little animal yelped and began to scrabble at James's chest, trying to get down.

"That settles it," said Mandy. "This one *must* be Licorice. He doesn't recognize you at all."

"No, he doesn't," said James. "He's trembling."

Mandy slid over the bike shed roof and dropped to the ground.

James looked down at the puppy shivering in his arms. Then he looked at Mandy, his eyes worried. "Let's get him back to Sarah as quickly as we can," he said. "Blackie must think we've abandoned him. I bet he's just as upset as Licorice by now!"

11

Puppy Playmates

Sarah lived at the far end of the village.

Mandy and James had nearly reached the front door of her house when it suddenly burst open and Sarah rushed out to meet them.

"Oh, you've found him!" she said, putting her arms out to take the puppy. "Oh, thank you for finding him. I was so worried." She buried her face in Licorice's soft fur. "Oh, Licorice!" she cried. "I thought you were lost. I didn't know what to do!"

Sarah cradled the little puppy in her arms and Licorice barked and began to lick her face. It was easy to see he was glad to be home.

Sarah lifted her head and looked at Mandy and James.

"Blackie is in the kitchen," she said. "I didn't understand why he was so unhappy at first. Then I realized he wasn't Licorice." She bit her lip. "You'd better come in," she said.

Mandy and James followed Sarah into the house. She led them into the kitchen. A small bundle of black fur jumped up from a basket on the floor and ran toward them, his tail wagging wildly.

"Blackie!" said James, picking him up.

Blackie's tail wagged so hard that it tickled James's chin. He giggled. "And here's Mandy," he said to the little dog.

Mandy went over and made a fuss of Blackie.

The little puppy nearly jumped out of James's arms in delight.

"I was so glad when I saw you coming up the path with Licorice," Sarah said. "And Blackie's glad, too."

Mandy turned to Sarah.

"When did you realize you had the wrong puppy?" she said.

Sarah blushed. "About five minutes ago," she said. "I really *did* think Blackie was Licorice. He didn't have a collar on when I found him."

She bit her lip again. "But I should have been more careful. It's just that I was in a hurry. My mom gets so angry if I keep her waiting."

James and Mandy looked at each other.

"Don't worry. It's all sorted out now," James said as Blackie tried to scramble up his chest.

"But I feel so bad," said Sarah.

"Don't," said Mandy. "Licorice and Blackie look so alike, anybody could make a mistake."

"But I should have checked," said Sarah. "Especially when you said the puppy I picked up was Blackie."

"Checked?" said James.

Sarah nodded. "Licorice has a little brown patch behind his left ear," she said. She looked miserable. "I suppose I *wanted* the puppy to be Licorice because I was in such a hurry. I'm sure you're mad at me."

Mandy shook her head. "No, we're not," she said. "Are we, James?"

James pushed his glasses up on his nose. "Of course we're not," he said. "I'm just glad to have Blackie back. It was awful to think he might be in danger."

"Danger?" said Sarah. "What do you mean?"

"Licorice scrambled up on top of that pile of wood in the playground," James said. "But Mandy climbed up and got him down."

Sarah's face went white. "Oh, no!" she said. "He is all right, isn't he?" And she looked down at the little puppy in her arms.

"Of course he's all right, Sarah," Mandy said. "Put him down and watch him run. You'll see he's okay."

Sarah put Licorice down on the floor. She began to look a little better as she watched him run around her feet.

"Uh-oh," said James. "Now Blackie wants to get down too."

James set Blackie down on the floor and the two puppies immediately began to roll about, playing. They ran around each other in tight circles, growling softly.

"Tell me exactly what happened," Sarah said.

James told her. Mandy was embarrassed. "I wasn't that brave, James," she said. "You're exaggerating."

But James wanted to let Sarah know what Mandy had done for her pet. When he had finished Sarah turned to Mandy. "Thank you so much, Mandy," she said. "I'm really sorry I ran off with Blackie." Sarah swallowed. "And I'm really sorry I left Licorice in danger like that."

"Or *any* puppy," said James.

Sarah nodded. "That's right," she said.

"Well," Mandy smiled, "everything is all right now so we'd better get going."

Sarah turned to her. "Don't go!" she said. Her face grew red. "I mean, can't you stay for a snack?"

Mandy and James looked at one another. Then they looked at the two puppies chasing each other around the kitchen table. The one in front suddenly stopped and turned, rearing up onto his hind legs.

"Look at Blackie!" said Mandy. Then she frowned. "Or is that Licorice?"

The three of them laughed.

"It's a good thing Licorice has a brown patch behind his ear," James said.

"They're really getting along well together, aren't they?" said Sarah as the two puppies rolled under the table in one furry black ball. She looked at Mandy and James. "I wish you *would* stay," she said. "The puppies are having such a good time."

"We *could* call home and let our parents know where we are," said James.

Mandy looked at Sarah. "If it's all right with your mom," she said.

Sarah nodded. "Of course it will be," she said. "Wait till I tell her how you saved Licorice!"

Mandy smiled. "Then we'd like to stay, wouldn't we, James?"

James nodded.

"And will you tell me everything I need to know to look after Licorice?" asked Sarah.

"Of course," said Mandy. "And I'll even lend you some books."

"Oh, thank you," said Sarah. "What's the first thing I should do?"

"That's easy," said James. "Get a collar from Mrs. McFarlane at the general store!"

Mandy looked down at the two puppies playing happily on the floor. They were getting along very well together.

"But whatever you do, don't get a red one," she said to Sarah. "We don't want another mix-up!"